THE MYSTERY OF
UFOs

Chris Oxlade

Heinemann Library
Chicago, Illinois

Customer Service 888-454-2279
Visit our website at www.heinemannraintree.com

Designed by Victoria Bevan and Q2A
Printed and bound in China by WKT

10 09 08 07 06
10 9 8 7 6 5 4 3 2 1

New edition ISBNs: 1-40348-338-8 (hardcover)
                   1-40348-347-7 (paperback)

The Library of Congress has cataloged the hardcover editions as follows:
Oxlade, Chris
        The mystery of UFOs / Chris Oxlade.
p.   cm. - (Can Science Solve?)
Includes bibliographical references and index
Summary: Discusses the phenomenon of unidentified flying objects, including notable sightings throughout history and possible explanations for them.
        ISBN 1-57572-806-0 (library binding)
1.   Unidentified flying objects—Sightings and encounters Juvenile literature. [1. Unidentified flying objects.] I. Title.
II. Series.
TL789.2.095   1999
001.942— dc21

                                        98-54488
                                        CIP
                                        AC

Acknowledgments
The author and publishers are grateful to the following for permission to reproduce copyright material:
Aviation Picture Library: p. 19; Mary Evans Picture Library: pp. 13 (upper), 24, 26, K Aarsleff p. 17, G Adamski p10, C Hart Jnr p. 9; Fortean Picture Library: pp. 6, 7, W Akins p28, B Askew p. 20, D Stacy p. 13 (Lower), F Taylor p. 23, A Vieira p. 29, P Villa p. 4; Science Photo Library: NASA p. 15, D Parker p. 18.

Cover picture of a flying saucer, reproduced with permission of Corbis/Roger Ball.

Every effort has been made to contact copyright holders of any material reproduced in this book. Any omissions will be rectified in subsequent printings if notice is given to the publisher.

The paper used to print this book comes from sustainable sources.

Some words are shown in bold, **like this**. You can find the definitions for these words in the glossary.

CONTENTS

UNSOLVED MYSTERIES

For hundreds of years, people have been interested in and puzzled by mysterious places, creatures, and events. Is there really a monster living in Loch Ness, in Scotland? Did the lost city of Atlantis ever exist? Are crop circles clever fakes or alien messages? Are UFOs tricks of the light, or actually vehicles from outer space? Some of these mysteries have baffled scientists, who have spent years trying to find the answer. But just how far can science go? Can it really explain the seemingly unexplainable? Are there some mysteries that science simply cannot solve? Read on, and make up your own mind . . .

This book tells you about the history of UFOs, retells eyewitness accounts, and looks at the different theories that attempt to explain them.

What is a UFO?

As you probably know, the letters *UFO* stand for "Unidentified Flying Object." Most people think that *UFO* is just another way of saying "alien spaceship," but it is not. A UFO is any light or object in the sky that cannot be explained. Some UFOs are not actually seen by the human eye, but are detected by **radar**, such as the radars used by air traffic controllers.

This is a photograph of a UFO taken by Paul Villa near Albuquerque, New Mexico.

It is important to remember that more than 90 percent of reported UFOs become IFOs: Identified Flying Objects. They might be aircraft, planets, or **weather balloons**, for example, but this still leaves many real UFOs. What are they? The most romantic theory is that UFOs are alien spacecraft spying on Earth. Some scientists believe that all UFOs are actually natural objects in the **atmosphere**, such as clouds. Others believe that they are **hallucinations** or **hoaxes**.

Most serious scientists dismiss UFOs as nonsense made up by eccentric (odd) people. This is perhaps not surprising, considering the wild and unbelievable stories of alien **abductions** in UFOs that so often appear in newspapers and on television programs. But is there anything science can do to help solve the mystery?

BEGINNINGS OF A MYSTERY

The UFO phenomenon first became international news in the late 1940s, but there are many reports of strange objects in the sky from well before that—even from thousands of years earlier. Some UFOlogists (people who study UFOs) think that the Star of Bethlehem, which was said to have appeared at the time of the birth of Jesus Christ, was a UFO. How else, they say, would it be able to move and stop, and indicate the exact building where Jesus was born?

Early UFOs

One of the earliest UFO sightings was made in China in 1914 B.C.E., where "ten flying suns" caused panic among the people. In 216 B.C.E., Roman troops saw several "ships in the sky" over Italy. There are several reports from Japan: in C.E. 1180 there was a "glowing vessel" in the sky; in 1235 there were strange moving lights overhead; and in 1749 thousands of Japanese people saw three huge flying objects for four days.

Some UFOlogists believe this 8,000-year-old painting from the Sahara Desert is of an alien space traveler.

UFO hotspots

There have been reports of UFOs from all over the world, but there tend to be more reports from some areas than others. Where are these UFO "hotspots?" Most tend to be in heavily populated areas in countries where people are interested in UFOs. More reports would be expected there because more people are looking for UFOs in the sky. Top hotspots include Gulf Breeze in Florida, Mexico City in Mexico, and Warminster in England.

In 1897 a farmer in Kansas said he saw a "huge, cigar-shaped object the length of a football field" descend from the sky into one of his fields. Inside the craft's glass cabin were six of the "strangest beings ever seen." The ship rose again, carrying away a cow on the end of a rope.

During World War II, pilots from both sides who flew over Europe occasionally saw small balls of light that seemed to follow their aircraft. The "foo fighters" (perhaps after the French word for fire, *feu*) have never been explained.

DID YOU SEE THAT?

Here are some of the most famous UFO sightings of recent times. There are more sightings and stories on page 10.

Kenneth Arnold, Mount Rainier, Washington state, 1947

Kenneth Arnold was flying over a mountain range searching for the wreck of a military transport plane when he saw a flash of light. Looking in the direction of the flash, he saw nine objects moving "like a saucer would if you skipped it across water." He estimated that they were about 66 feet (20 meters) across and were flying at more than 1,250 miles (2,000 kilometers) per hour—three times faster than any aircraft of the time could manage. Arnold's is one of the most famous sightings of all because the press took his description and coined the phrase *flying saucer*. Within days of its appearance in the newspapers, there were a huge number of UFO reports from all across the United States.

Classes of encounter

U.S. UFOlogist Dr. J. Allen Hynek came up with this classification for encounters with UFOs and aliens:

- CE1 (Close Encounter of the First Kind): When a UFO is spotted at a distance, such as a light or object in the sky.

- CE2: When a UFO leaves a sign of its presence, such as marks on the ground.

- CE3: When the eyewitness sees alien creatures inside or outside a UFO.

- CE4: When a person is abducted by aliens.

- CE5: When a person talks or communicates with an alien.

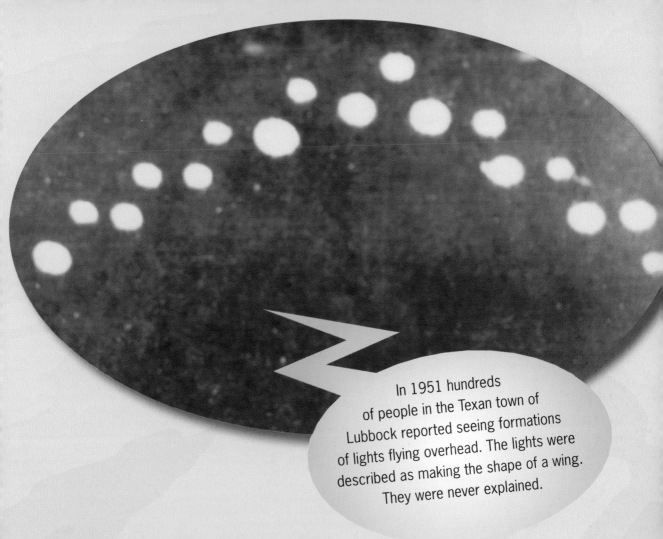

In 1951 hundreds of people in the Texan town of Lubbock reported seeing formations of lights flying overhead. The lights were described as making the shape of a wing. They were never explained.

UFO on film, New Zealand, 1978

An Australian TV reporter and a film crew were on a plane looking for a UFO that had been spotted a few days earlier. They saw, and filmed, several bright lights in the sky and an object with a bright base and dome that kept pace with the plane. **Radar** on the ground confirmed that an object was there, but the sighting was never explained.

The Trident sighting, Portugal, 1976

A British Airways Trident aircraft was south of Lisbon, Portugal, when the crew heard air traffic control reports of a UFO on their radar. Out of the windows, the crew and passengers of the Trident saw a bright light and a long, cigar-shaped object approaching the light. The crews of two other aircraft confirmed the sighting. An hour later, on the Trident's return flight, the crew detected by radar an object the size of a supertanker in the same place, but saw nothing.

MEETING THE ALIENS

On these pages, you can read reports of UFOs that include meetings with aliens and **abductions** by aliens. Mostly, people who claim to have been abducted find it hard to remember what happened to them. All they know is that several hours are missing from their memories and something odd happened. Hypnosis (a trance-like sleep) can often help them to remember.

This is one of George Adamski's many photographs of UFOs. This one is a "Venusian interplanetary carrier," photographed through an astronomical telescope.

All in the mind?

Psychologists suggest that alien abductions are not real events. They believe that people who claim they have been abducted have just imagined it all while they are in a dream-like state, which the psychologists call sleep paralysis. This can also happen just before you fall fully asleep, and it can make you feel awake while you dream.

George Adamski, California, 1952

This celebrated case is the first example of a human possibly meeting an alien. Adamski claims that on one afternoon in 1952, while he was watching and photographing a flying saucer, a human-like alien approached him. Using hand gestures and telepathy (the ability to communicate with thoughts), the alien told Adamski that he was from Venus. The incident was witnessed from a distance by two families. This meeting was the first of many—Adamski claims to have been taken by flying saucer on trips to Mars, Saturn, and Jupiter, where he met inhabitants of each planet. Adamski has no proof of his encounters.

Betty and Barney Hill, New Hampshire, 1961

This was the first widely reported case of people being abducted by aliens. The Hills were driving home late at night when they saw a bright light ahead. The light got brighter and closer and appeared to be moving. Eventually they stopped the car and Barney got out and approached the object, which was hovering above the ground. Seeing a dozen "people" inside, he fled back to the car. The couple drove off, but were in a "sedated" (calm or sleepy) state for some time. Ten days later, Betty began to have nightmares in which aliens took them from their car and examined them in a spaceship. She became convinced that she was remembering real events. Under hypnosis, both Betty and Barney recalled the abduction, but nothing can be proved.

IT'S OFFICIAL

Today, the world's governments tend to take little interest in UFO reports from the public, but the military does investigate UFOs that its radars detect. In the past, however, they took reports more seriously. In the United States in the 1940s, 1950s, and 1960s, the Air Force was responsible for investigating UFOs. At the time, the Cold War was at its height, and the American people were concerned about an attack from the Soviet Union. Some UFOs were thought to be bizarre new Soviet aircraft. The Air Force attempted to explain UFOs—and to avoid admitting that they could not account for some sightings.

Project Blue Book

Between 1952 and 1969, the U.S. Air Force kept a record of all UFO reports it received. This record was called Project Blue Book. In all, it listed 12,318 sightings. All were investigated and most were explained, except for 701 sightings that remained a mystery.

Men in black

You may have heard of the 1998 movie "Men in Black," but do you know what men in black were? They were men in dark suits and dark glasses who supposedly visited UFO eyewitnesses and investigators and threatened them to keep quiet about their experiences. Some people claim that they were agents of the U.S. government; others say they were aliens themselves!

The conspiracy theory

Many UFOlogists are convinced that the governments of the world, especially the U.S. government, have convincing evidence that some UFOs are actually alien spacecraft. They claim that there is a cover-up, mainly by the CIA (the U.S. government-run Central Intelligence Agency), to prevent panic. In the U.S., a group of engineers and scientists called the Condon Committee was set up by the Air Force to investigate unsolved UFO sightings. They concluded that none were alien spacecraft—a conclusion denied by UFOlogists.

This debris, found in 1947 near Roswell Air Force Base, New Mexico, is claimed to be the remains of either a **weather balloon** (by the U.S. Air Force) or a flying saucer (by many UFOlogists).

There are also rumored reports that several astronauts have encountered UFOs, including one report that Neil Armstrong saw a fleet of huge spacecraft on the Moon during the *Apollo 11* trip in 1969. **Conspiracy theorists** say that the astronauts were told to keep quiet and that the published photographs of the Moon landings were faked by **NASA** in a movie studio in order to cover up this fact.

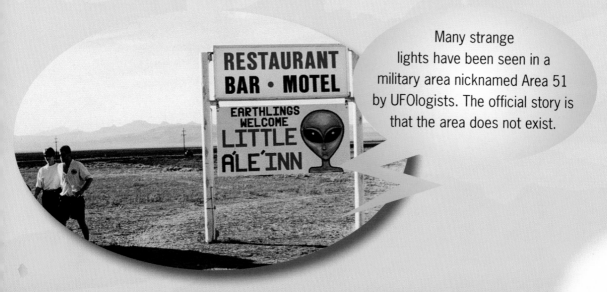

RESTAURANT
BAR · MOTEL

EARTHLINGS
WELCOME
LITTLE
ALE'INN

Many strange lights have been seen in a military area nicknamed Area 51 by UFOlogists. The official story is that the area does not exist.

ARE WE ALONE?

The case for UFOs being alien spacecraft would seem more believable if we could find evidence that there was actually intelligent life in other parts of the universe. So, how likely is other life, and how could we find out if it was there?

The chances of life

We know that Earth is the only planet in our **solar system** where there is life. The chances of intelligent life evolving on Earth must have been very small, but it happened.

Astronomers know that there are billions of stars like our Sun in our **galaxy,** and there are billions more galaxies in the universe. They have found evidence of large planets **orbiting** our neighboring stars (the stars wobble slightly as the planets move around them), although they have never seen them. If this is the case, it is not unreasonable to think that there may be many Earth-like planets out there where life may have evolved, too.

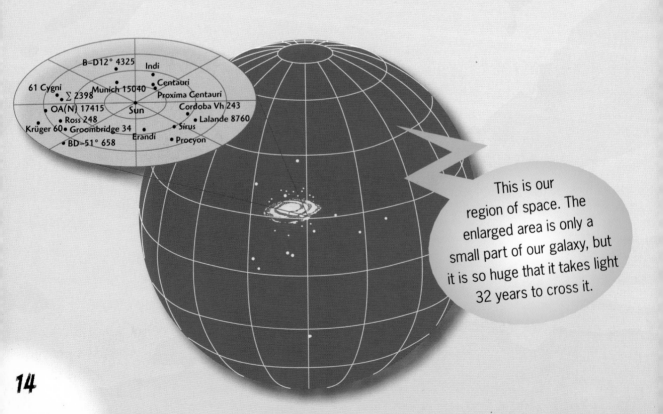

This is our region of space. The enlarged area is only a small part of our galaxy, but it is so huge that it takes light 32 years to cross it.

Signals from Earth

Trying to contact life on other planets presents one huge problem: the distances involved. Radio signals travel at the speed of light (186,400 miles, or 300,000 kilometers, per second), but they still take more than four years to reach even our nearest star neighbor. Then, you have to wait for the reply to come back at the same speed. Many of the radio signals we use on Earth for communications are spreading into space and may be detected by other beings. In 1973 a simple **binary** radio message was sent toward a cluster of stars called M13, in the hope that there is life around one of the many stars there. It will take 25,000 years to reach the cluster.

The plaque on the space probes *Pioneer 10* and *11* would help intelligent forms of life find Earth if they ever found the probes.

Listening up

In 1982 a group of Russian and U.S. scientists set up a project known as SETI (Search for **Extra-Terrestrial** Intelligence) to look for radio signals coming from outer space using a radio telescope. They have listened to thousands of stars without finding anything, but there are millions more to go.

In 1977 U.S. astronomer Bob Dixon detected a 37-second-long powerful radio signal from the area of the **constellation** Sagittarius. However, the signal was random and has never been repeated.

TRAVEL TO THE STARS

If we assume that there is other intelligent life in the universe, could we ever visit it? More importantly for the explanation of UFOs, could members of that intelligent life build a spacecraft and visit us?

The age of civilization

Astronomers think that our **solar system** was formed about 4.5 billion years ago. The oldest **fossils** ever found are of simple sea-living organisms that are three billion years old. Creatures began to inhabit the land about 500 million years ago and human-like creatures evolved about four million years ago. Farming began about 10,000 years ago, and industry began about 300 years ago. Computers have been developed in the last 40 years. From this, you can see that the pace of technological change is getting faster and faster. As the 21st century starts, our knowledge of science seems enormous, but it may just be the tip of the iceberg.

Gods or aliens?

There are theories that aliens visited Earth in ancient times and communicated with people, teaching them technologies way ahead of their time. The main pieces of evidence for this theory are archaeological finds called out-of-place artifacts (OOPARTS)—objects that are thousands of years old, but have modern technologies in them. One example is an 1,800-year-old ceramic pot found in Iraq that acts as a battery. Another is a 5.5-inch- (14-centimeter-) long glider made in 200 B.C.E. that flies perfectly.

Now, imagine a planet in another solar system where things are one million years ahead of us. What sort of scientific knowledge and technology would they have? Would it be advanced enough to build a spacecraft capable of crossing the huge expanse of space between their world and ours? At the speed that our current spacecraft travel, about 25,000 miles (40,000 kilometers) per hour, it would take about 27,000 years to cover the four light-years to our nearest star. (A light-year is the distance light travels in a year—about 5.9 trillion miles, or 9.5 trillion kilometers.) But with a spacecraft capable of one quarter the speed of light, about 155 million miles (250 million kilometers) per hour, it would take about sixteen years.

These lines in Peru are claimed to be landing areas for UFOs that visited Earth thousands of years ago.

IDENTIFIED OBJECTS

Most of the UFOs reported by the public can actually be put down to perfectly normal objects or **optical illusions** created by the weather. On these pages, you can find out which objects are often mistaken for UFOs. On pages 20–23, you can find out about tricks of the weather.

Real flying objects

Aircraft are often reported as UFOs, especially at night when only their lights are visible. Helicopter lights confuse people because helicopters can hover still in the air and move in all directions. Other UFO-like objects are hot-air balloons, airships, **weather balloons**, kites, and birds. Weather balloons are very confusing because they rise very high into the **atmosphere** and are often silver and reflect the sunlight. These shapes are sometimes also distorted by **mirages** (see page 21).

This is a type of weather balloon called a meduse. You can see how it could be reported as a flying saucer.

Some UFOs are seen on **radar** screens rather than with the naked eye. However, radars can also be fooled. Thick clouds, flocks of birds, and places where hot and cold air meet can give false radar reflections that look like large objects on a screen.

In the U.S., some reports of bizarre shapes in the sky have been explained as experimental aircraft, such as this "stealth" fighter.

Space objects

Some UFOs are actually in outer space, but they are objects that **astronomers** know all about. They can be mistaken for strange lights in the sky because they reflect sunlight brightly. For example, the planet Venus, which is the brightest planet in the sky, is often visible in the evening or morning. **Satellites** in low **orbits** around Earth look like tiny, fast-moving lights when the Sun shines on them. Rockets taking off have also been mistaken for UFOs. Objects that fly into Earth's atmosphere, such as **meteors** and bits of old rockets, burn up and cause a streak of light.

WEIRD WEATHER

It is thought that natural events in Earth's **atmosphere** can explain more than 90 percent of the sightings of strange lights and shapes in the sky. In fact, many UFO researchers are beginning to ignore "lights in the sky" reports because they are almost certainly atmospheric phenomena.

Cloud shapes

How many times have you seen clouds that look like people's faces or animals? Clouds can also be mistaken for classic flying saucers, especially a type of cloud called a lenticular cloud. These are formed when wind blows over mountaintops and is made to flow up and down like a wave. As the air rises, saucer-shaped clouds are formed.

Stranger still are noctilucent clouds. These are very high-**altitude** clouds, formed up to 50 miles (80 kilometers) up (ten times higher than normal clouds), and made up of ice particles. After sunset, the Sun's rays light up the clouds, making them look like glowing purple spaceships.

Perfectly natural clouds can look amazingly like UFOs.

Mirages

A **mirage** is an image in the sky of an object that is not really there. People have even seen cities on the opposite side of seas appear in the sky because of mirages. Mirages are caused by changes in the temperature in different layers of air. Light rays coming from objects can be bent up or down as they pass through the layers of air. You might have seen "puddles" on roads on hot summer days. What you are actually seeing is a mirage of the sky.

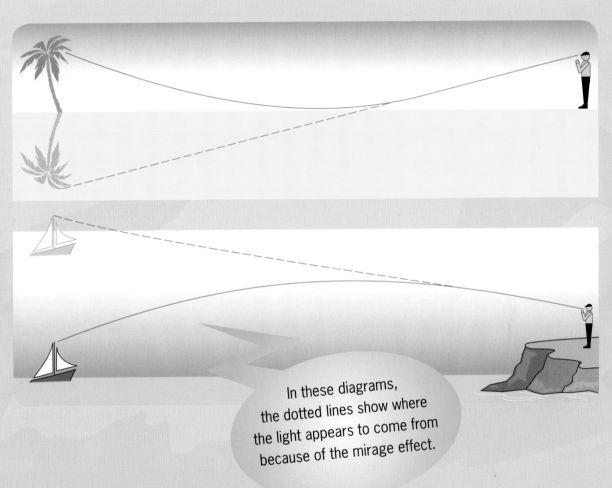

In these diagrams, the dotted lines show where the light appears to come from because of the mirage effect.

Sun and Moon dogs

In certain atmospheric conditions, rays of light from the Sun or Moon that would normally pass you by are bent inside clouds. This has the effect of making two more Suns or Moons appear at each side of the real one, looking like hovering lights in the sky. These **optical illusions** are called Sun or Moon dogs.

LIGHTS OR LIGHTNING?

Lightning is the cause of many reports of "spaceship lights" in the sky. Lightning is caused by **static electricity** that builds up in clouds jumping to the ground. A huge electric current passes through the air, creating a spark-like glow. Sheet lightning (when the whole sky seems to light up) is sometimes thought to be the flash of spaceship engines.

Balls of light and fireballs

One of the strangest and spookiest of all weather **phenomena** is called ball lightning. It normally happens just after a thunderstorm, and it looks like a glowing ball of light the size of a soccer ball or smaller. Eyewitnesses have seen ball lightning under apparently "intelligent" control—floating through their houses, following their cars, drifting through their aircraft, and even shooting up into the air. It is no wonder that people link ball lightning with spacecraft and aliens. Scientists do not yet understand how ball lightning forms or travels, but they do know that it is an electrical phenomenon, because engineers working on electricity power lines have occasionally seen ball lightning form during their work.

Meteor showers

In November 2005 there were numerous sightings of fireballs in the sky over Germany. They led to several reports of UFO sightings. However, scientists believe that the fireballs were caused by a **meteor** shower. A meteor shower is seen when small rocks from space burn up on contact with Earth's **atmosphere**.

Glowing vortices

British tornado and whirlwind expert Dr. Terence Meaden believes that many UFO reports are linked to another mystery—the formation of crop circles, which are circular patterns that mysteriously appear in fields of crops. His "plasma vortex theory" suggests that spinning, glowing bodies of electrically charged air create crop circles—and also look like glowing spacecraft in the sky. They move in an "intelligent" way that is similar to ball lightning and create humming sounds.

Many believe that crop circles are messages left by aliens. Dr. Terence Meaden believes that both phenomena can be explained by his "plasma vortex theory."

FAMOUS FAKES

As for all mysterious happenings, there are plenty of UFO **hoaxes**. They do not help the cause of the people who believe that UFOs are alien spacecraft. They come in two categories: hoax reports of sightings and **abductions** and fake photographs. Of course, many reports of alien abductions are probably not real, but rather are dreams that people think are true. They are not purposeful fakes.

Group of UFOs, Sheffield, England, 1962

In 1962 two schoolboys from Sheffield, England, claimed that they had a photograph of a formation of five UFOs flying over Sheffield. The newspapers printed it, calling it the "best UFO photograph ever," and UFOlogists exhibited it as proof of an alien visit. Several more UFO sightings were reported soon after. Ten years later, one of the boys admitted that the photograph was a fake. They had painted five saucer shapes on a sheet of glass and taken a photograph through it! Amazingly, UFO supporters were reluctant to believe that the photograph was a hoax.

This photograph was taken in 1962 of UFOs over Sheffield, England. It was a fake.

This is the famous Mexico City photograph, suspected to be a fake.

Fake aliens

There are not only fake photographs of UFOs, but also of aliens that are claimed to have come from spacecraft that have crashed to Earth. One of the most famous is of an alien that is supposed to have survived a crash near Mexico City in the 1950s. It is highly likely to be a fake because the photograph is fuzzy, plus no trace has been found of the alien's body or its spacecraft.

Spotting the fake

Some UFO photographs are obvious fakes, but some are more difficult to spot. Photographic experts are normally able to tell whether a photograph has been "doctored" after it has been taken by looking at the film's grain under a microscope. Two things to look for in a fake photograph are the difference in detail between the landscape and the UFO and whether the UFO is blurred—this often suggests it is a model. Modern **digital photography** and computer photo-editing will make fakes easier to do and more difficult to spot.

WHY FAKE UFOS?

There are certainly many made-up stories about UFOs
and plenty of fake photos of alien spacecraft. But what is
the point of making up stories and faking photographs?
The Sheffield schoolboys and the fakers of the Mexico City
photograph probably did it just for fun or to impress their
friends. The obvious reason is to try to make some money.

Selling your story

Is there any money to be made out of faking UFOs?
Probably, if you sell a convincing story to a national newspaper.
Certain newspapers would be delighted to have an "exclusive" alien
story. This might have worked in the 1950s, but today, it has to be
very convincing and original because of the thousands of reports
of UFOs and alien **abductions** that happen every year. Perhaps
a good photo of a flying saucer or alien creature would do the
trick? Again, it would have to be very good because of the number
of fake photographs
created using **digital
photography** and
computer graphics.
However, there are
some UFOlogists who
have done well by
publishing their
thoughts in books.

A good hoax could get
you into print—in this case in the
magazine *Fate*.

Is it all a hoax?

Some people claim that all stories of little green men are made up and that all photographs of alien spacecraft (not necessarily photographs of lights in the sky) and their occupants are **hoaxes**. This may well be true, but it is hard to believe that all UFO reports are made up, especially when many come from apparently reliable witnesses.

How to fake a UFO picture

For fun, you could try faking your own flying saucer photograph. Try throwing saucer-shaped objects into the air in front of the camera. You could also take photographs through a window in which there is a reflection of a light or through a window with spaceship images stuck onto it. Or, try scanning and combining photographs on a computer.

Creating UFO pictures is easy with a computer. People are now difficult to convince, since they are used to seeing composite (combined) pictures like this in ads.

background photograph

scanner

The two images combined using graphics software.

Flying saucer created using
3D computer software.

WHAT DO YOU THINK?

So, can science really solve the mystery of UFOs? It's certain that science, especially meteorology, can explain many UFO reports. In the future, when we understand more about electrical effects in the atmosphere, such as ball lightning, it may be possible to explain many more. But, at the moment, there are still many UFOs that science can't explain.

Are we being visited by intelligent life from other planets?

Sounds convincing . . .

• Many of the eyewitness reports of sophisticated UFOs come from reliable witnesses such as pilots and military personnel.

• There are billions of other planets in the universe. It seems unlikely that Earth is the only one where intelligent life has evolved.

• Although humans have not yet found a way to visit other planets, life on other planets could be much more technologically advanced than Earth.

But what about . . . ?

• Scientists' attempts to contact life on other planets have not been successful, so far.

• If aliens are visiting us, why have they not made themselves known to all of us?

This shows a UFO over Charlotte, South Carolina, in 1971.

Aliens about to invade or a flash of lightning? This is a UFO over Sao Paulo, Brazil, in 1984.

There is no doubt that there are UFOs—objects in the sky that we cannot identify. But are they from other planets? With the help of science, we are beginning to find other planets in the universe, but at the moment we don't have the technology to reach them and find out for certain.

What about the other theories? Do you think any of them might be true? Look at the list of theories below and think about the pros and cons of each. Decide which you think are the most convincing.

- Most UFOs are normal, explainable objects such as helicopters or **weather balloons**.

- UFOs are objects in space, such as nearby planets, that reflect the Sun's light brightly.

- Clouds and other weather conditions, such as ball lightning, can explain many UFOs.

- Governments and the military can explain many UFOs but choose not to, possibly because they are experimental technology.

- All UFO sightings are fakes or **hallucinations**.

What are your conclusions? Are there theories you can dismiss without further investigation? Do you have any theories of your own? Try to keep an open mind. Remember that science is constantly evolving and new discoveries are being made all the time. Just because something can't be proved scientifically now, it doesn't mean this will always be the case.

GLOSSARY

abduction kidnapping

altitude height of an object above Earth's surface, normally measured in feet

astronomer person who studies space and the objects in space

atmosphere layer of air that surrounds Earth

binary simple code made up of the digits 1 and 0, or on and off signals

Cold War period that began after World War II and lasted into the 1960s, when there was a political struggle with the United States and countries of Western Europe on one side and the countries of Eastern Europe, headed by the Soviet Union, on the other side

conspiracy theorist person who says that a group of people have plotted together to keep information from the public

constellation group of stars that seem to form a pattern when seen from Earth

digital photography photography using a camera that stores photographs as numbers inside memory chips instead of on film. The photographs can easily be copied onto a computer and edited on screen.

extra-terrestrial describes any object or being that does not come from Earth

fossil remains of an ancient animal or plant (normally a prehistoric one) that has been buried under the ground and has gradually turned to rock

galaxy enormous cloud of stars in space that can contain billions of stars. Our own galaxy is called the Milky Way.

hallucination when you think you see or hear something that is not really there

hoax something that tricks people

meteor piece of rock, dust, or ice from space that hurtles into Earth's atmosphere, where friction with the air makes it glow white hot. It makes a streak of light across the sky.

meteorology study of Earth's atmosphere and what causes the weather

mirage optical illusion that makes objects appear in mid-air. Mirages are caused when light is bent through layers of warm air near the ground on hot days.

NASA (National Aeronautics and Space Administration) organization in the U.S. that controls the U.S. space program

optical illusion image seen by the eye that is not what is seems

orbit path that an object, such as a moon or a satellite, takes as it moves around a star or a planet

phenomenon remarkable or unexplained happening

radar device that can detect objects in the air. It sends out radio waves and detects any that return because they bounce off objects. It shows the objects on a screen.

satellite object that moves around a star, planet, or moon in an orbit

solar system Sun and its family of planets and moons

static electricity electricity that builds up on objects that are rubbed together. For example, your clothes build up static electricity when they rub together, which makes them attract dust and hair.

weather balloon balloon that carries equipment to measure weather conditions

Find Out More

You can find out more about UFOs in books and on the Internet. Use a search engine such as www.yahooligans.com to search for information. A search for "UFO" will bring back lots of results, but it may be difficult to find the information you want. Try narrowing your search to look for some of the people and ideas mentioned in this book, such as "George Adamski" or "SETI."

More Books to Read

Brooks, Philip. *Invaders from Outer Space: Real-Life Stories of UFOs*. New York: DK, 1999.

Mason, Paul. *Forensic Files: Investigating UFOs*. Chicago: Heinemann Library, 2004.

Townsend, John. *Out There? Mysterious Encounters*. Chicago: Raintree, 2004.

Websites

www.seti.org: The official website of the Search for Extra-Terrestrial Intelligence (SETI).

INDEX